THIS BOOK
BELONGS TO:

_____

_____

A
CHILD'S GARDEN
OF VERSES

CHILDREN'S CLASSICS

This unique series of Children's Classics™ features accessible and highly readable texts paired with the work of talented and brilliant illustrators of bygone days to create fine editions for today's parents and children to rediscover and treasure. Besides being a handsome addition to any home library, this series features faux leather spines stamped in gold, full-color illustrations, and high-quality acid-free paper that will enable these books to be passed from one generation to the next.

Adventures of Huckleberry Finn
The Adventures of Tom Sawyer
Aesop's Fables
Alice's Adventures in Wonderland
Andersen's Fairy Tales
Anne of Avonlea
Anne of Green Gables
At the Back of the North Wind
Black Beauty
The Call of the Wild
A Child's Book of Country Stories
A Child's Book of Stories
A Child's Book of Stories from
   Many Lands
A Child's Christmas
A Child's Garden of Verses
A Christmas Carol and Other
   Christmas Stories
Cinderella and Other Classic
   Italian Fairy Tales
The Complete Mother Goose
Goldilocks and the Three Bears and
   Other Classic English Fairy Tales
Great Dog Stories
Grimm's Fairy Tales
Hans Brinker *or* The Silver Skates
Heidi
The Hound of the Baskervilles
Joan of Arc

The Jungle Book
Just So Stories
Kidnapped
King Arthur and His Knights
Lancelot: The Adventures of King
   Arthur's Most Celebrated Knight
The Legend of Pocahontas
A Little Child's Book of Stories
Little Men
A Little Princess
Little Women
Peter Pan
Pollyanna
The Prince and the Pauper
Rebecca of Sunnybrook Farm
Robin Hood
Robinson Crusoe
The Secret Garden
The Sleeping Beauty and Other
   Classic French Fairy Tales
The Swiss Family Robinson
Tales from Shakespeare
Tales of Pirates and Buccaneers
Through the Looking Glass and
   What Alice Found There
Treasure Island
A Very Little Child's Book of Stories
The Wind in the Willows
The Wonderful Wizard of Oz

A CHILD'S GARDEN OF VERSES
ROBERT LOVIS STEVENSON

WITH ILLVSTRATIONS BY
JESSIE WILLCOX SMITH

CHILDREN'S CLASSICS
New York • Avenel, New Jersey

Preface copyright © 1985 by Random House Value Publishing, Inc.
All rights reserved.

This edition is published by Children's Classics, an imprint and trademark of Random House Value Publishing, Inc., 40 Engelhard Avenue, Avenel, New Jersey 07001.

Printed and bound in the United States of America

Library of Congress Cataloging-in-Publication Data

Stevenson, Robert Louis, 1850-1894.
     A child's garden of verses / Robert Louis Stevenson ; illustrated by Jessie Willcox   Smith.
       p. cm.
     Summary: A collection of poems evoking the world and feelings of childhood.
     ISBN 0-517-12397-5
     1. Children's poetry, Scottish. [1. Scottish poetry.]
I. Smith, Jessie Willcox, ill. II. Title.
PR5489.C5 1995
821'.8—dc20

                            95-17610
                               CIP
                               AC

8 7 6 5 4 3 2 1

CONTENTS

CONTENTS

CONTENTS

THE CHILD ALONE

GARDEN DAYS

ENVOYS

TO ALISON CUNNINGHAM

FROM HER BOY

FOR the long nights you lay awake
 And watched for my unworthy sake:
For your most comfortable hand
That led me through the uneven land:
For all the story-books you read:
For all the pains you comforted:

For all you pitied, all you bore,
In sad and happy days of yore :—
My second Mother, my first Wife,
The angel of my infant life —
From the sick child, now well and old,
Take, nurse, the little book you hold !

And grant it, Heaven, that all who read
May find as dear a nurse at need,
And every child who lists my rhyme,
In the bright, fireside, nursery clime,
May hear it in as kind a voice
As made my childish days rejoice !

R. L. S.

LIST OF COLOR ILLUSTRATIONS

FOREWORD

More than a century has passed since the first publication of Robert Louis Stevenson's *A Child's Garden of Verses*, eighty years since Jessie Willcox Smith illustrated his verses with her magic brush. Both Stevenson and Smith were possessed of the same rare skill of evoking the sensual memories of childhood's innocent enchantments. How fitting that we should now be offered the gift of this new printing of an edition that married their special talents, as a special remembrance of a perfect pairing.

Some lucky children have enchanted childhoods where days are spent in simple pleasures and pursuits. Robert Louis Stevenson did not have such a childhood. He was born and grew up in Edinburgh, the only son of a wealthy civil engineer; however, he was a sickly child, and the climate of Edinburgh was ill-suited to his constitution. His dedication of *A Child's Garden of Verses* to Alison Cunningham, his nurse, is the only glimpse he gives us of his less than perfect early years:

From the sick child, now well and old . . .

FOREWORD

Stevenson's ill health, which later developed into tuberculosis, fostered an appreciation of the simplicity of childhood. Each moment, each ritual, each routine activity is presented in his verses with such captivating candor that we are encircled and embraced with forgotten images of beauty and gentleness. When, at the age of thirty-two, he began to work on *A Child's Garden of Verses* (first called *Penny Whistles*), he was able to recall with an incredible accuracy the feelings, both sensual and intellectual, of the little child. Seldom has a poet captured more perfectly the adult's sweet nostalgia or the child's budding awareness of nature, time, and the occupations that fill a happy childhood.

In these rhymes Stevenson moves back and forth, to and fro, from present to past, from adult to child. Sometimes he is the adult, thinking out loud about childhood, as in "A Thought," "The Unseen Playmate," "Nest Eggs," and "Whole Duty of Children." At other times he is the adult or the older child recalling a past experience, as in "The Land of Counterpane"; and often he is the teacher, as in "Good and Bad Children" and "Looking-Glass River." But most often, he becomes the child he was; the past comes alive in the present, and he is once again living his childhood. This last perspective creates the sharpest images through its immediacy, as in "Winter-time":

> Late lies the wintry sun a-bed,
> A frosty, fiery sleepy-head;
> Blinks but an hour or two; and then,
> A blood-red orange, sets again.

He does not describe the sun setting in a language a child would use; but with his words he is able to share with the reader a verbal recreation of a winter sunset experienced through the eyes of a child.

FOREWORD

He does the same sort of thing in "A Good Boy":

No ugly dream shall fright my mind,
no ugly sight my eyes,
But slumber hold me tightly
till I waken in the dawn,
And hear the thrushes singing
in the lilacs round the lawn.

The details he uses to convey the promise of peaceful sleep and happy awakening could not be identified or described ahead of time by a child; but we, as adults, can grasp them with a sigh and a smile evoked by the total sweetness of the image they transmit.

It doesn't really matter where you grow up—city, country, or somewhere in between—you and your children can intuitively own the sights, the smells, the tastes, the sounds of Stevenson's garden. His constant traveling as an adult, both for reasons of ill health and in pursuit of love and adventure, took him from Edinburgh to the countryside of Suffolk in England, to the French Riviera, to the United States (where he traveled, following his future wife, Fanny Osbourne), to California—Monterey and San Francisco—to Davos, Switzerland, and Bournemouth on the coast of England, all before he began to write *A Child's Garden of Verses*. Some of the verses seem to have been influenced by his new vistas. The meadows seem more English than Scottish ("Pirate Story"); the "dark brown" of the river in "Where Go the Boats?" recalls the Mississippi; and "The Lamplighter" could well be illuminating the London streets. But we know because he tells us so in "The Land of Story Books" that, in his imagination, he traveled far from home long before he took his first railway-carriage ride.

It was in 1894, the year that Stevenson died, that Jessie Willcox

Smith first enrolled at the Drexel Institute of the Arts and Sciences in Philadelphia (now Drexel University) to pursue her studies in illustration. Smith, the youngest of four children of a Philadelphia investment broker, was first drawn by her love of children toward a career as a kindergarten teacher. However, while studying to become a teacher, she discovered her talent for drawing and turned in that direction instead. She became an immensely successful illustrator and built a reputation largely on her singular ability to portray the nuances of childhood experiences and children's personalities.

In her gloriously detailed illustrations for *A Child's Garden of Verses* we are given a delightful sampling of her work. She shows us real children. They are not glorified and angel-faced beauties, but they are beautiful in their originality; their features are not symmetrical to a fault. The children are natural—busy and unposed. Each child she paints belongs to someone. It is as if we had walked into a friend's home or garden during the early years of the twentieth century and encountered the children. We feel at home in her art. The line drawings effortlessly capture the energy and unselfconscious freedom of movement of children that adults so often envy. Then, too, we have the wonderful glimpses of the child totally immersed in the contemplation of a puddle, a shadow, an orange slice. The interiors of the houses are cozy. The gardens dazzle our senses and invite us to return again to stay.

One especially wonderful thing about this book is that it is appropriate for parents to read aloud to very young children. Its simple little verses catch the imagination of every child who has ever loved to go up in a swing or play with his shadow. Both the author's and the illustrator's love of and pleasure in every little corner of nature's bounty will introduce the child to the excitement of doing active things, the endless pleasure of watching people, the security of observing rituals and routines. One also hopes that it might succeed in drawing today's children, and the generations who follow them, out and away from the flatlands of television to the real and sensual loveliness that the world has to offer.

In any time capsule intended to show future civilizations what our world was like at its best, I would hope for the inclusion of Robert Louis Stevenson's *A Child's Garden of Verses*. It is more than one hundred years old—and it has centuries more to go!

PATRICIA BARRETT PERKINS

Baltimore, Maryland

A
CHILD'S GARDEN
OF VERSES

I

BED IN SUMMER

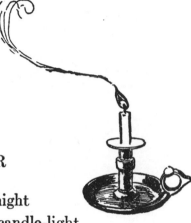

IN winter I get up at night
And dress by yellow candle-light.
In summer, quite the other way,
I have to go to bed by day.

I have to go to bed and see
The birds still hopping on the tree,
Or hear the grown-up people's feet
Still going past me in the street.

And does it not seem hard to you,
When all the sky is clear and blue,
And I should like so much to play,
To have to go to bed by day?

Mary   Hans

II

A THOUGHT

IT is very nice to think
    The world is full of meat and drink,
    With little children saying grace
    In every Christian kind of place.

Biddy   Fifine

III

AT THE SEA–SIDE

WHEN I was down beside the sea
    A wooden spade they gave to me
      To dig the sandy shore.

My holes were empty like a cup.
In every hole the sea came up,
    Till it could come no more.

IV

YOUNG NIGHT-THOUGHT

ALL night long and every night,
When my mama puts out the light,
I see the people marching by,
As plain as day, before my eye.

Armies and emperors and kings,
All carrying different kinds of things,
And marching in so grand a way,
You never saw the like by day.

So fine a show was never seen
At the great circus on the green;
For every kind of beast and man
Is marching in that caravan.

At first they move a little slow,
But still the faster on they go,
And still beside them close I keep
Until we reach the town of Sleep.

V

WHOLE DUTY OF CHILDREN

A CHILD should always say what's true
And speak when he is spoken to,
And behave mannerly at table;
At least as far as he is able.

VI

RAIN

THE rain is raining all around,
It falls on field and tree,
It rains on the umbrellas here,
And on the ships at sea.

VII

PIRATE STORY

THREE of us afloat in the meadow by the swing,
   Three of us aboard in the basket on the lea.
Winds are in the air, they are blowing in the spring,
   And waves are on the meadow like the waves there
      are at sea.

Where shall we adventure, to-day that we're afloat,
   Wary of the weather and steering by a star?
Shall it be to Africa, a-steering of the boat,
   To Providence, or Babylon, or off to Malabar?

Hi! but here's a squadron a-rowing on the sea —
   Cattle on the meadow a-charging with a roar!
Quick, and we'll escape them, they're as mad as they can be,
   The wicket is the harbour and the garden is the shore.

VIII

FOREIGN LANDS

U P into the cherry tree
    Who should climb but little me?
    I held the trunk with both my hands
    And looked abroad on foreign lands.

I saw the next door garden lie,
Adorned with flowers, before my eye,
And many pleasant places more
That I had never seen before.

I saw the dimpling river pass
And be the sky's blue looking-glass;
The dusty roads go up and down
With people tramping in to town.

If I could find a higher tree
Farther and farther I should see,
To where the grown-up river slips
Into the sea among the ships,

10

To where the roads on either hand
Lead onward into fairy land,
Where all the children dine at five,
And all the playthings come alive.

IX

WINDY NIGHTS

WHENEVER the moon and stars are set,
    Whenever the wind is high,
    All night long in the dark and wet,
  A man goes riding by.
Late in the night when the fires are out,
Why does he gallop and gallop about?

Whenever the trees are crying aloud,
  And ships are tossed at sea,
By, on the highway, low and loud,
  By at the gallop goes he.
By at the gallop he goes, and then
By he comes back at the gallop again.

X

TRAVEL

I SHOULD like to rise and go
Where the golden apples grow;—
Where below another sky
Parrot islands anchored lie,
And, watched by cockatoos and goats,
Lonely Crusoes building boats;—
Where in sunshine reaching out
Eastern cities, miles about,
Are with mosque and minaret
Among sandy gardens set,
And the rich goods from near and **far**
Hang for sale in the bazaar;—
Where the Great Wall round China goes,
And on one side the desert blows,
And with bell and voice and drum,
Cities on the other hum;—
Where are forests, hot as fire,
Wide as England, tall as a spire,
Full of apes and cocoa-nuts
And the negro hunters' huts;—

13

Where the knotty crocodile
Lies and blinks in the Nile,
And the red flamingo flies
Hunting fish before his eyes ; —
Where in jungles, near and far,
Man-devouring tigers are,
Lying close and giving ear
Lest the hunt be drawing near,
Or a comer-by be seen
Swinging in a palanquin ; —
Where among the desert sands
Some deserted city stands,
All its children, sweep and prince,
Grown to manhood ages since,
Not a foot in street or house,
Not a stir of child or mouse,
And when kindly falls the night,
In all the town no spark of light.
There I'll come when I'm a man
With a camel caravan ;
Light a fire in the gloom
Of some dusty dining-room ;
See the pictures on the walls,
Heroes, fights, and festivals ;
And in a corner find the toys
Of the old Egyptian boys.

BED IN SUMMER
(Page 3)

FOREIGN LANDS
(Page 10)

XI

SINGING

O F speckled eggs the birdie sings
And nests among the trees ;
The sailor sings of ropes and things
In ships upon the seas.

The children sing in far Japan,
The children sing in Spain ;
The organ with the organ man
Is singing in the rain.

XII

LOOKING FORWARD

WHEN I am grown to man's estate
I shall be very proud and great,
And tell the other girls and boys
Not to meddle with my toys.

16

XIII

A GOOD PLAY

WE built a ship upon the stairs
  All made of the back-bedroom chairs,
  And filled it full of sofa pillows
  To go a-sailing on the billows.

We took a saw and several nails,
And water in the nursery pails;
And Tom said, "Let us also take
An apple and a slice of cake;" —
Which was enough for Tom and me
To go a-sailing on, till tea.

We sailed along for days and days
And had the very best of plays;
But Tom fell out and hurt his knee,
So there was no one left but me.

17

XIV

WHERE GO THE BOATS?

DARK brown is the river,
    Golden is the sand.
     It flows along for ever,
With trees on either hand.

Green leaves a-floating,
  Castles of the foam,
Boats of mine a-boating —
  Where will all come home?

On goes the river
  And out past the mill,
Away down the valley,
  Away down the hill.

Away down the river,
  A hundred miles or more,
Other little children
  Shall bring my boats ashore.

XV

AUNTIE'S SKIRTS

WHENEVER Auntie moves around,
Her dresses make a curious sound,
They trail behind her up the floor,
And trundle after through the door.

19

XVI

THE LAND OF COUNTERPANE

WHEN I was sick and lay a-bed,
    I had two pillows at my head,
    And all my toys beside me lay
    To keep me happy all the day.

And sometimes for an hour or so
I watched my leaden soldiers go,
With different uniforms and drills,
Among the bed-clothes, through the hills;

And sometimes sent my ships in fleets
All up and down among the sheets;
Or brought my trees and houses out,
And planted cities all about.

I was the giant great and still
That sits upon the pillow-hill,
And sees before him, dale and plain,
The pleasant land of counterpane.

XVII

THE LAND OF NOD

FROM breakfast on through all the day
At home among my friends I stay,
But every night I go abroad
Afar into the land of Nod.

All by myself I have to go,
With none to tell me what to do —
All alone beside the streams
And up the mountain-sides of dreams.

The strangest things are there for me,
Both things to eat and things to see,
And many frightening sights abroad
Till morning in the land of Nod.

Try as I like to find the way,
I never can get back by day,
Nor can remember plain and clear
The curious music that I hear.

XVIII

MY SHADOW

I HAVE a little shadow that goes in and out with me,
And what can be the use of him is more than I can see.
He is very, very like me from the heels up to the head;
And I see him jump before me, when I jump into my bed.

The funniest thing about him is the way he likes to grow —
Not at all like proper children, which is always very slow;
For he sometimes shoots up taller like an india-rubber ball,
And he sometimes gets so little that there's none of him at all.

He hasn't got a notion of how children ought to play,
And can only make a fool of me in every sort of way.

He stays so close beside me, he's a coward you can see;
I'd think shame to stick to nursie as that shadow sticks to
    me!

One morning, very early, before the sun was up,
I rose and found the shining dew on every buttercup;
But my lazy little shadow, like an arrant sleepy-head,
Had stayed at home behind me and was fast asleep in bed.

XIX

SYSTEM

EVERY night my prayers I say,
　　And get my dinner every day;
　　And every day that I've been good,
I get an orange after food.

The child that is not clean and neat,
With lots of toys and things to eat,
He is a naughty child, I'm sure —
Or else his dear papa is poor.

XX

A GOOD BOY

I WOKE before the morning, I was happy all the day,
   I never said an ugly word, but smiled and stuck to
   play.

And now at last the sun is going down behind the wood,
And I am very happy, for I know that I've been good.

My bed is waiting cool and fresh, with linen smooth and fair
And I must be off to sleepsin-by, and not forget my prayer.

I know that, till to-morrow I shall see the sun arise,
No ugly dream shall fright my mind, no ugly sight my eyes.

But slumber hold me tightly till I waken in the dawn,
And hear the thrushes singing in the lilacs round the lawn.

XXI

ESCAPE AT BEDTIME

THE lights from the parlour and kitchen shone out
    Through the blinds and the windows and bars;
    And high overhead and all moving about,
There were thousands of millions of stars.
There ne'er were such thousands of leaves on a tree,
  Nor of people in church or the Park,
As the crowds of the stars that looked down upon me,
  And that glittered and winked in the dark.

The Dog, and the Plough, and the Hunter, and all,
  And the star of the sailor, and Mars,
These shone in the sky, and the pail by the wall
  Would be half full of water and stars.

They saw me at last, and they chased me with cries,
    And they soon had me packed into bed;
But the glory kept shining and bright in my eyes,
    And the stars going round in my head.

XXII

MARCHING SONG

BRING the comb and play upon it!
   Marching, here we come!
   Willie cocks his highland bonnet,
Johnnie beats the drum.

Mary Jane commands the party,
  Peter leads the rear;
Feet in time, alert and hearty,
  Each a Grenadier!

All in the most martial manner
   Marching double-quick;
While the napkin, like a banner,
   Waves upon the stick!

Here's enough of fame and pillage,
   Great commander Jane!
Now that we've been round the village,
   Let's go home again.

XXIII

THE COW

THE friendly cow all red and white,
   I love with all my heart:
She gives me cream with all her might,
   To eat with apple-tart.

She wanders lowing here and there,
   And yet she cannot stray,
All in the pleasant open air,
   The pleasant light of day;

And blown by all the winds that pass
  And wet with all the showers,
She walks among the meadow grass
  And eats the meadow flowers.

XXIV

HAPPY THOUGHT

THE world is so full of a number of things,
I'm sure we should all be as happy as kings.

XXV

THE WIND

I SAW you toss the kites on high
 And blow the birds about the sky;
 And all around I heard you pass,
Like ladies' skirts across the grass —
 O wind, a-blowing all day long,
 O wind, that sings so loud a song!

I saw the different things you did,
But always you yourself you hid.
I felt you push, I heard you call,
I could not see yourself at all —
 O wind, a-blowing all day long,
 O wind, that sings so loud a song!

O you that are so strong and cold,
O blower, are you young or old?
Are you a beast of field and tree,

Or just a stronger child than me?
O wind, a-blowing all day long,
O wind, that sings so loud a song!

XXVI

KEEPSAKE MILL

OVER the borders, a sin without pardon,
　　Breaking the branches and crawling below,
　　Out through the breach in the wall of the garden,
Down by the banks of the river, we go.

Here is the mill with the humming of thunder,
　　Here is the weir with the wonder of foam,
Here is the sluice with the race running under —
　　Marvellous places, though handy to home!

Sounds of the village grow stiller and stiller,
　　Stiller the note of the birds on the hill;
Dusty and dim are the eyes of the miller,
　　Deaf are his ears with the moil of the mill.

Years may go by, and the wheel in the river
　　Wheel as it wheels for us, children, to-day,
Wheel and keep roaring and foaming for ever
　　Long after all of the boys are away.

Home from the Indies and home from the ocean,
  Heroes and soldiers we all shall come home;
Still we shall find the old mill wheel in motion,
  Turning and churning that river to foam.

You with the bean that I gave when we quarrelled,
  I with your marble of Saturday last,
Honoured and old and all gaily apparelled,
  Here we shall meet and remember the past.

XXVII

GOOD AND BAD CHILDREN

CHILDREN, you are very little,
And your bones are very brittle;
If you would grow great and stately,
You must try to walk sedately.

You must still be bright and quiet,
And content with simple diet;
And remain, through all bewild'ring,
Innocent and honest children.

39

Happy hearts and happy faces,
Happy play in grassy places —
That was how, in ancient ages,
Children grew to kings and sages.

But the unkind and the unruly,
And the sort who eat unduly,
They must never hope for glory —
Theirs is quite a different story!

Cruel children, crying babies,
All grew up as geese and gabies,
Hated, as their age increases,
By their nephews and their nieces.

XXVIII

FOREIGN CHILDREN

LITTLE Indian, Sioux or Crow,
    Little frosty Eskimo,
    Little Turk or Japanee,
      Oh! don't you wish that you were me?

You have seen the scarlet trees
And the lions over seas;
You have eaten ostrich eggs,
And turned the turtles off their legs.

41

Such a life is very fine,
But it's not so nice as mine:
You must often, as you trod,
Have wearied *not* to be abroad.

You have curious things to eat,
I am fed on proper meat;
You must dwell beyond the foam,
But I am safe and live at home.
   Little Indian, Sioux or Crow,
   Little frosty Eskimo,
   Little Turk or Japanee,
Oh! don't you wish that you were me?

XXIX

THE SUN TRAVELS

THE sun is not a-bed, when I
  At night upon my pillow lie;
  Still round the earth his way he takes,
  And morning after morning makes.

While here at home, in shining day,
We round the sunny garden play,
Each little Indian sleepy-head
Is being kissed and put to bed.

And when at eve I rise from tea,
Day dawns beyond the Atlantic Sea;
And all the children in the West
Are getting up and being dressed.

XXX

THE LAMPLIGHTER

MY tea is nearly ready and the sun has left the sky.
   It's time to take the window to see Leerie going
      by;
For every night at teatime and before you take your seat,
With lantern and with ladder he comes posting up the street.

Now Tom would be a driver and Maria go to
   sea,
And my papa's a banker and as rich as he can
   be;
But I, when I am stronger and can choose what
   I'm to do,
O Leerie, I'll go round at night and light the
   lamps with you!

For we are very lucky, with a lamp before the
   door,
And Leerie stops to light it as he lights so many
   more;
And oh! before you hurry by with ladder and
   with light;
O Leerie, see a little child and nod to him to-
   night!

XXXI

THE MOON

THE moon has a face like the clock in the hall;
She shines on thieves on the garden wall,
On streets and fields and harbour quays,
And birdies asleep in the forks of the trees.

The squalling cat and the squeaking mouse,
The howling dog by the door of the house,
The bat that lies in bed at noon,
All love to be out by the light of the moon.

But all of the things that belong to the day
Cuddle to sleep to be out of her way;
And flowers and children close their eyes
Till up in the morning the sun shall arise.

THE LAND OF COUNTERPANE
(Page 20)

LOOKING-GLASS RIVER
(Page 52)

XXXII

MY BED IS A BOAT

MY bed is like a little boat;
　　　Nurse helps me in when I embark;
　　　She girds me in my sailor's coat
And starts me in the dark.

At night, I go on board and say
　　Good-night to all my friends on shore;
I shut my eyes and sail away
　　And see and hear no more.

And sometimes things to bed I take,
    As prudent sailors have to do ;
Perhaps a slice of wedding-cake,
    Perhaps a toy or two.

All night across the dark we steer ;
    But when the day returns at last,
Safe in my room, beside the pier,
    I find my vessel fast.

XXXIII

THE SWING

HOW do you like to go up in a swing,
    Up in the air so blue?
    Oh, I do think it the pleasantest thing
Ever a child can do!

Up in the air and over the wall,
  Till I can see so wide,
Rivers and trees and cattle and all
  Over the countryside —

Till I look down on the garden green,
  Down on the roof so brown —
Up in the air I go flying again,
  Up in the air and down!

XXXIV

TIME TO RISE

A BIRDIE with a yellow bill
Hopped upon the window sill,
Cocked his shining eye and said:
"Ain't you 'shamed, you sleepy-head!"

51

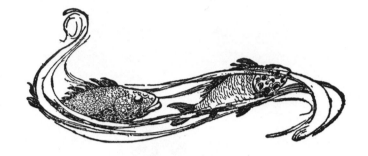

XXXV

LOOKING–GLASS RIVER

SMOOTH it glides upon its travel,
  Here a wimple, there a gleam —
    O the clean gravel!
    O the smooth stream!

Sailing blossoms, silver fishes,
  Paven pools as clear as air —
    How a child wishes
    To live down there!

We can see our coloured faces
  Floating on the shaken pool
    Down in cool places,
    Dim and very cool;

Till a wind or water wrinkle,
  Dipping marten, plumping trout,
    Spreads in a twinkle
    And blots all out.

See the rings pursue each other;
  All below grows black as night,
    Just as if mother
    Had blown out the light!

Patience, children, just a minute —
  See the spreading circles die;
    The stream and all in it
    Will clear by-and-by.

XXXVI

FAIRY BREAD

COME up here, O dusty feet!
　　Here is fairy bread to eat.
　　Here in my retiring room,
Children, you may dine
On the golden smell of broom
　　And the shade of pine;
And when you have eaten well,
Fairy stories hear and tell.

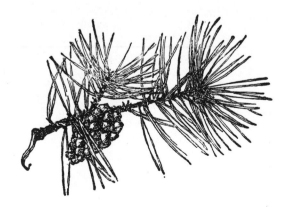

XXXVII

FROM A RAILWAY CARRIAGE

FASTER than fairies, faster than witches,
　　Bridges and houses, hedges and ditches;
　　And charging along like troops in a battle
All through the meadows the horses and cattle:
All of the sights of the hill and the plain
Fly as thick as driving rain;
And ever again, in the wink of an eye,
Painted stations whistle by.

Here is a child who clambers and scrambles,
All by himself and gathering brambles;
Here is a tramp who stands and gazes;
And there is the green for stringing the daisies
Here is a cart run away in the road
Lumping along with man and load;
And here is a mill, and there is a river:
Each a glimpse and gone for ever!

XXXVIII

WINTER–TIME

LATE lies the wintry sun a-bed,
A frosty, fiery sleepy-head;
Blinks but an hour or two; and then,
A blood-red orange, sets again.

Before the stars have left the skies,
At morning in the dark I rise;
And shivering in my nakedness,
By the cold candle, bathe and dress.

Close by the jolly fire I sit
To warm my frozen bones a bit;
Or with a reindeer-sled, explore
The colder countries round the door.

When to go out, my nurse doth wrap
Me in my comforter and cap;
The cold wind burns my face, and blows
Its frosty pepper up my nose.

Black are my steps on silver sod;
Thick blows my frosty breath abroad;
And tree and house, and hill and lake,
Are frosted like a wedding-cake.

XXXIX

THE HAYLOFT

THROUGH all the pleasant meadow-side
　　The grass grew shoulder-high,
　　Till the shining scythes went far and wide
And cut it down to dry.

Those green and sweetly smelling crops
　　They led in waggons home;
And they piled them here in mountain tops
　　For mountaineers to roam.

Here is Mount Clear, Mount Rusty-Nail,
  Mount Eagle and Mount High ; —
The mice that in these mountains dwell,
  'No happier are than I !

Oh, what a joy to clamber there,
  Oh, what a place for play,
With the sweet, the dim, the dusty air,
  The happy hills of hay !

XL

FAREWELL TO THE FARM

THE coach is at the door at last;
The eager children, mounting fast
And kissing hands, in chorus sing:
Good-bye, good-bye, to everything!

To house and garden, field and lawn,
The meadow-gates we swang upon,
To pump and stable, tree and swing,
Good-bye, good-bye, to everything!

And fare you well for evermore,
O ladder at the hayloft door,
O hayloft where the cobwebs cling,
Good-bye, good-bye, to everything!

Crack goes the whip, and off we go ;
The trees and houses smaller grow ;
Last, round the woody turn we swing:
Good-bye, good-bye, to everything !

THE HAYLOFT
(Page 59)

NORTH-WEST PASSAGE
(Page 63)

XLI

NORTH–WEST PASSAGE

1. GOOD–NIGHT

WHEN the bright lamp is carried in,
   The sunless hours again begin;
   O'er all without, in field and lane,
The haunted night returns again.

Now we behold the embers flee
About the firelit hearth; and see
Our faces painted as we pass,
Like pictures, on the window-glass.

Must we to bed indeed? Well then,
Let us arise and go like men,
And face with an undaunted tread
The long black passage up to bed.

Farewell, O brother, sister, sire!
O pleasant party round the fire!
The songs you sing, the tales you tell,
Till far to-morrow, fare ye well!

2. SHADOW MARCH

All round the house is the jet-black night;
  It stares through the window-pane;
It crawls in the corners, hiding from the light,
  And it moves with the moving flame.

Now my little heart goes a-beating like a drum,
  With the breath of the Bogie in my hair;
And all round the candle the crooked shadows come,
  And go marching along up the stair.

The shadow of the balusters, the shadow of the lamp,
  The shadow of the child that goes to bed —
All the wicked shadows coming, tramp, tramp, tramp,
  With the black night overhead.

3. IN PORT

Last, to the chamber where I lie
My fearful footsteps patter nigh,
And come from out the cold and gloom
Into my warm and cheerful room.

There, safe arrived, we turn about
To keep the coming shadows out,
And close the happy door at last
On all the perils that we past.

Then, when mamma goes by to bed,
She shall come in with tip-toe tread,
And see me lying warm and fast
And in the Land of Nod at last.

THE CHILD ALONE

I

THE UNSEEN PLAYMATE

WHEN children are playing alone on the green,
    In comes the playmate that never was seen.
    When children are happy and lonely and good,
    The Friend of the Children comes out of the
        wood.

Nobody heard him and nobody saw,
His is a picture you never could draw,
But he's sure to be present, abroad or at home,
When children are happy and playing alone.

He lies in the laurels, he runs on the grass,
He sings when you tinkle the musical glass;
Whene'er you are happy and cannot tell why,
The Friend of the Children is sure to be by!

He loves to be little, he hates to be big,
'T is he that inhabits the caves that you dig;
'T is he when you play with your soldiers of tin
That sides with the Frenchmen and never can win.

'T is he, when at night you go off to your bed,
Bids you go to your sleep and not trouble your head;
For wherever they're lying, in cupboard or shelf,
'T is he will take care of your playthings himself!

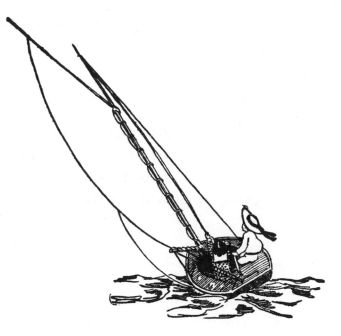

II

MY SHIP AND I

O IT'S I that am the captain of a tidy little ship,
　　Of a ship that goes a-sailing on the pond;
　And my ship it keeps a-turning all around and all
　　　about;
But when I'm a little older, I shall find the secret out
How to send my vessel sailing on beyond.

For I mean to grow as little as the dolly at the helm,
 And the dolly I intend to come alive;
And with him beside to help me, it's a-sailing I shall go,
It's a-sailing on the water, when the jolly breezes blow
 And the vessel goes a divie-divie-dive.

O it's then you'll see me sailing through the rushes and the
  reeds,
 And you'll hear the water singing at the prow;
For beside the dolly sailor, I'm to voyage and explore,
To land upon the island where no dolly was before,
 And to fire the penny cannon in the bow.

III

MY KINGDOM

DOWN by a shining water well
    I found a very little dell,
        No higher than my head.
The heather and the gorse about
In summer bloom were coming out,
        Some yellow and some red.

I called the little pool a sea;
The little hills were big to me;
  For I am very small.
I made a boat, I made a town,
I searched the caverns up and down,
  And named them one and all.

And all about was mine, I said,
The little sparrows overhead,
  The little minnows too.
This was the world and I was king;
For me the bees came by to sing,
  For me the swallows flew.

I played there were no deeper seas,
Nor any wider plains than these,
  Nor other kings than me.
At last I heard my mother call
Out from the house at evenfall,
  To call me home to tea.

And I must rise and leave my dell,
And leave my dimpled water well,
  And leave my heather blooms.
Alas! and as my home I neared,
How very big my nurse appeared.
  How great and cool the rooms!

V

MY TREASURES

THESE nuts, that I keep in the back of the nest
Where all my lead soldiers are lying at rest,
Were gathered in autumn by nursie and me
In a wood with a well by the side of the sea.

This whistle we made (and how clearly it sounds!)
By the side of a field at the end of the grounds.
Of a branch of a plane, with a knife of my own,
It was nursie who made it, and nursie alone!

The stone, with the white and the yellow and grey,
We discovered I cannot tell *how* far away;
And I carried it back although weary and cold,
For though father denies it, I'm sure it is gold.

But of all my treasures the last is the king,
For there's very few children possess such a thing;
And that is a chisel, both handle and blade,
Which a man who was really a carpenter made.

VI

BLOCK CITY

WHAT are you able to build with your blocks?
Castles and palaces, temples and docks.
Rain may keep raining, and others go roam,
But I can be happy and building at home.

Let the sofa be mountains, the carpet be sea,
There I'll establish a city for me:
A kirk and a mill and a palace beside,
And a harbour as well where my vessels may ride.

Great is the palace with pillar and wall,
A sort of a tower on the top of it all,
And steps coming down in an orderly way
To where my toy vessels lie safe in the bay.

This one is sailing and that one is moored:
Hark to the song of the sailors on board!
And see, on the steps of my palace, the kings
Coming and going with presents and things!

Now I have done with it, down let it go!
All in a moment the town is laid low.
Block upon block lying scattered and free,
What is there left of my town by the sea?

Yet as I saw it, I see it again,
The kirk and the palace, the ships and the men,
And as long as I live and where'er I may be,
I'll always remember my town by the sea.

THE LAND OF STORY-BOOKS

AT evening when the lamp is lit,
　　Around the fire my parents sit;
　　They sit at home and talk and sing,
　　And do not play at anything.

Now, with my little gun, I crawl
All in the dark along the wall,
And follow round the forest track
Away behind the sofa back.

There, in the night, where none can spy,
All in my hunter's camp I lie,
And play at books that I have read
Till it is time to go to bed.

These are the hills, these are the woods,
These are my starry solitudes;
And there the river by whose brink
The roaring lions come to drink.

I see the others far away
As if in firelit camp they lay,
And I, like to an Indian scout,
Around their party prowled about.

So, when my nurse comes in for me,
Home I return across the sea,
And go to bed with backward looks
At my dear land of Story-books.

VIII

ARMIES IN THE FIRE

THE lamps now glitter down the street;
Faintly sound the falling feet;
And the blue even slowly falls
About the garden trees and walls.

Now in the falling of the gloom
The red fire paints the empty room:
And warmly on the roof it looks,
And flickers on the backs of books.

Armies march by tower and spire
Of cities blazing, in the fire ; —
Till as I gaze with staring eyes,
The armies fade, the lustre dies.

Then once again the glow returns ;
Again the phantom city burns ;
And down the red-hot valley, lo !
The phantom armies marching go !

Blinking embers, tell me true
Where are those armies marching to,
And what the burning city is
That crumbles in your furnaces !

IX

THE LITTLE LAND

WHEN at home alone I sit,
  And am very tired of it,
  I have just to shut my eyes
To go sailing through the skies —
To go sailing far away
To the pleasant Land of Play;
To the fairy land afar
Where the Little People are;
Where the clover-tops are trees,
And the rain-pools are the seas,
And the leaves, like little ships,
Sail about on tiny trips;
And above the daisy tree
 Through the grasses,
High o'erhead the Bumble Bee
 Hums and passes.

In that forest to and fro
I can wander, I can go;
See the spider and the fly,
And the ants go marching by,
Carrying parcels with their feet
Down the green and grassy street.
I can in the sorrel sit
Where the ladybird alit.
I can climb the jointed grass
   And on high
See the greater swallows pass
   In the sky,
And the round sun rolling by
Heeding no such things as I.

Through that forest I can pass
Till, as in a looking-glass,
Humming fly and daisy tree
And my tiny self I see,
Painted very clear and neat
On the rain-pool at my feet.
Should a leaflet come to land
Drifting near to where I stand,
Straight I'll board that tiny boat
Round the rain-pool sea to float.

Little thoughtful creatures sit
On the grassy coasts of it;
Little things with lovely eyes
See me sailing with surprise.

Some are clad in armour green —
(These have sure to battle been!) —
Some are pied with ev'ry hue,
Black and crimson, gold and blue;
Some have wings and swift are gone; —
But they all look kindly on.

When my eyes I once again
Open, and see all things plain:
High bare walls, great bare floor;
Great big knobs on drawer and door;
Great big people perched on chairs,
Stitching tucks and mending tears,
Each a hill that I could climb,
And talking nonsense all the time —
O dear me,
That I could be
A sailor on the rain-pool sea,
A climber in the clover tree,
And just come back, a sleepy-head,
Late at night to go to bed.

GARDEN DAYS

I

NIGHT AND DAY

WHEN the golden day is done,
    Through the closing portal,
    Child and garden, flower and sun,
Vanish all things mortal.

As the blinding shadows fall
    As the rays diminish,
Under evening's cloak, they all
    Roll away and vanish.

Garden darkened, daisy shut,
    Child in bed, they slumber —
Glow-worm in the highway rut,
    Mice among the lumber.

In the darkness houses shine,
　　Parents move with candles;
Till on all, the night divine
　　Turns the bedroom handles.

Till at last the day begins
　　In the east a-breaking,
In the hedges and the whins
　　Sleeping birds a-waking.

In the darkness shapes of things,
　　Houses, trees and hedges,
Clearer grow; and sparrow's wings
　　Beat on window ledges.

These shall wake the yawning maid;
　　She the door shall open —
Finding dew on garden glade
　　And the morning broken.

There my garden grows again
　　Green and rosy painted,
As at eve behind the pane
　　From my eyes it fainted.

Just as it was shut away,
　　Toy-like, in the even,
Here I see it glow with day
　　Under glowing heaven.

PICTURE-BOOKS IN WINTER
(Page 77)

THE FLOWERS
(Page 98)

Every path and every plot,
   Every bush of roses,
Every blue forget-me-not
   Where the dew reposes.

"Up!" they cry, "the day is come
   On the smiling valleys:
We have beat the morning drum;
   Playmate, join your allies!"

II

NEST EGGS

BIRDS all the sunny day
　　Flutter and quarrel
　　Here in the arbour-like
Tent of the laurel.

Here in the fork
　　The brown nest is seated;
Four little blue eggs
　　The mother keeps heated.

While we stand watching her
　　Staring like gabies,
Safe in each egg are the
　　Bird's little babies.

Soon the frail eggs they shall
  Chip, and upspringing
Make all the April woods
  Merry with singing.

Younger than we are,
  O children, and frailer,
Soon in blue air they'll be,
  Singer and sailor.

We, so much older,
  Taller and stronger,
We shall look down on the
  Birdies no longer.

They shall go flying
  With musical speeches
High overhead in the
  Tops of the beeches.

In spite of our wisdom
  And sensible talking,
We on our feet must go
  Plodding and walking.

III

THE FLOWERS

ALL the names I know from nurse:
Gardener's garters, Shepherd's purse,
Bachelor's buttons, Lady's smock,
And the Lady Hollyhock.

Fairy places, fairy things,
Fairy woods where the wild bee wings,
Tiny trees for tiny dames —
These must all be fairy names!

Tiny woods below whose boughs
Shady fairies weave a house;
Tiny tree-tops, rose or thyme,
Where the braver fairies climb!

Fair are grown-up people's trees,
But the fairest woods are these;
Where, if I were not so tall,
I should live for good and all.

IV

SUMMER SUN

GREAT is the sun, and wide he goes
Through empty heaven without repose;
And in the blue and glowing days
More thick than rain he showers his rays.

Though closer still the blinds we pull
To keep the shady parlour cool,
Yet he will find a chink or two
To slip his golden fingers through.

The dusty attic spider-clad
He, through the keyhole, maketh glad;
And through the broken edge of tiles
Into the laddered hay-loft smiles.

Meantime his golden face around
He bares to all the garden ground,
And sheds a warm and glittering look
Among the ivy's inmost nook.

Above the hills, along the blue,
Round the bright air with footing true,
To please the child, to paint the rose,
The gardener of the World, he goes.

THE DUMB SOLDIER

WHEN the grass was closely mown,
Walking on the lawn alone,
In the turf a hole I found,
And hid a soldier underground.

Spring and daisies came apace;
Grasses hide my hiding place;
Grasses run like a green sea
O'er the lawn up to my knee.

Under grass alone he lies,
Looking up with leaden eyes,
Scarlet coat and pointed gun,
To the stars and to the sun.

When the grass is ripe like grain,
When the scythe is stoned again,
When the lawn is shaven clear,
Then my hole shall reappear.

I shall find him, never fear,
I shall find my grenadier;
But for all that's gone and come,
I shall find my soldier dumb.

He has lived, a little thing,
In the grassy woods of spring;
Done, if he could tell me true,
Just as I should like to do.

He has seen the starry hours
And the springing of the flowers;
And the fairy things that pass
In the forests of the grass.

In the silence he has heard
Talking bee and ladybird,
And the butterfly has flown
O'er him as he lay alone.

Not a word will he disclose,
Not a word of all he knows.
I must lay him on the shelf,
And make up the tale myself.

VI

AUTUMN FIRES

IN the other gardens
    And all up the vale,
   From the autumn bonfires
See the smoke trail!

Pleasant summer over
  And all the summer flowers,
The red fire blazes,
  The grey smoke towers.

Sing a song of seasons!
　Something bright in all!
Flowers in the summer,
　Fires in the fall!

VII

THE GARDENER

THE gardener does not love to talk,
  He makes me keep the gravel walk;
  And when he puts his tools away,
  He locks the door and takes the key.

Away behind the currant row,
Where no one else but cook may go,
Far in the plots, I see him dig,
Old and serious, brown and big.

106

He digs the flowers, green, red, and blue,
Nor wishes to be spoken to.
He digs the flowers and cuts the hay,
And never seems to want to play.

Silly gardener! summer goes,
And winter comes with pinching toes,
When in the garden bare and brown
You must lay your barrow down.

Well now, and while the summer stays,
To profit by these garden days
O how much wiser you would be
To play at Indian wars with me!

VIII

HISTORICAL ASSOCIATIONS

DEAR Uncle Jim, this garden ground
    That now you smoke your pipe around,
    Has seen immortal actions done
    And valiant battles lost and won.

Here we had best on tip-toe tread,
While I for safety march ahead,
For this is that enchanted ground
Where all who loiter slumber sound.

Here is the sea, here is the sand,
Here is simple Shepherd's Land,
Here are the fairy hollyhocks,
And there arc Ali Baba's rocks.

But yonder, see! apart and high,
Frozen Siberia lies; where I,
With Robert Bruce and William Tell,
Was bound by an enchanter's spell.

ENVOYS

I

TO WILLIE AND HENRIETTA

IF two may read aright
    These rhymes of old delight
    And house and garden play,
You too, my cousins, and you only, **may.**

    You in a garden green
    With me were king and queen,
    Were hunter, soldier, tar,
And all the thousand things that children are.

    Now in the elders' seat
    We rest with quiet feet,
    And from the window-bay
We watch the children, our successors, **play.**

"Time was," the golden head
Irrevocably said;
But time which none can bind,
While flowing fast away, leaves love behind.

II

TO MY MOTHER

YOU too, my mother, read my rhymes
For love of unforgotten times,
And you may chance to hear once more
The little feet along the floor.

III

TO AUNTIE

*C*HIEF *of our aunts — not only I,*
    But all your dozen of nurselings cry —
    What did the other children do?
    And what were childhood, wanting you?

IV

TO MINNIE

THE red room with tne giant bed
    Where none but elders laid their head;
    The little room where you and I
Did for awhile together lie
And, simple suitor, I your hand
In decent marriage did demand;
The great day nursery, best of all,
With pictures pasted on the wall
And leaves upon the blind

A pleasant room wherein to wake
And hear the leafy garden shake
And rustle in the wind —
And pleasant there to lie in bed
And see the pictures overhead —
The wars about Sebastopol,
The grinning guns along the wall,
The daring escalade,
The plunging ships, the bleating sheep,
The happy children ankle-deep
And laughing as they wade;
All these are vanished clean away,
And the old manse is changed to-day;
It wears an altered face
And shields a stranger race.
The river, on from mill to mill,
Flows past our childhood's garden still;
But ah! we children never more
Shall watch it from the water-door.
Below the yew — it still is there —
Our phantom voices haunt the air
As we were still at play,
And I can hear them call and say:
"*How far is it to Babylon?*"

Ah, far enough, my dear,
Far, far enough from here —
Yet you have farther gone!

"*Can I get there by candlelight?*"
So goes the old refrain.
I do not know — perchance you might —
But only, children, hear it right,
Ah, never to return again!
The eternal dawn, beyond a doubt,
Shall break on hill and plain,
And put all stars and candles out
Ere we be young again.

To you in distant India, these
I send across the seas,
Nor count it far across.
For which of us forgets
The Indian cabinets,
The bones of antelope, the wings of albatross,
The pied and painted birds and beans,
The junks and bangles, beads and screens,
The gods and sacred bells,
And the loud-humming, twisted shells!
The level of the parlour floor
Was honest, homely, Scottish shore;
But when we climbed upon a chair,
Behold the gorgeous East was there!
Be this a fable; and behold
Me in the parlour as of old,
And Minnie just above me set
In the quaint Indian cabinet!

Smiling and kind, you grace a shelf
Too high for me to reach myself.
Reach down a hand, my dear, and take
These rhymes for old acquaintance' sake!

V

TO MY NAME–CHILD

1

SOME day soon this rhyming volume, if you learn with
        proper speed,
  Little Louis Sanchez, will be given you to read.
Then shall you discover, that your name was printed down
By the English printers, long before, in London town.

In the great and busy city where the East and West are
      met,
All the little letters did the English printer set;
While you thought of nothing, and were still too young to
      play,
Foreign people thought of you in places far away.

Now that you have spelt your lesson, lay it down and go
    and play,
Seeking shells and seaweed on the sands of Monterey,
Watching all the mighty whalebones, lying buried by the
    breeze,
Tiny sandpipers, and the huge Pacific seas.

And remember in your playing, as the sea-fog rolls to you,
Long ere you could read it, how I told you what to do;
And that while you thought of no one, nearly half the world
    away
Some one thought of Louis on the beach of Monterey!

Ay, and while you slept, a baby, over all the English lands
Other little children took the volume in their hands ;
Other children questioned, in their homes across the seas:
Who was little Louis, won't you tell us, mother, please?

VI

TO ANY READER

As from the house your mother sees
    You playing round the garden trees,
    So you may see, if you will look
Through the windows of this book,
Another child, far, far away,
And in another garden, play.
But do not think you can at all,
By knocking on the window, call
That child to hear you. He intent
Is all on his play-business bent.